THERE'S A LIZARD IN MY LETTERBOX!

WRITTEN AND ILLUSTRATED

BY

PATTI GIBBONS

2

I dedicate this book to my daughter for the inspiration, my son and daughter-in-law for their encouragement, my grandchildren for their love, and my husband for his humor.

THIS BOOK BELONGS TO

____

THERE'S A LIZARD IN MY LETTERBOX.
I SAW HIM THERE TODAY.
WHEN I REACHED IN TO GET MY MAIL,
HE DIDN'T RUN AWAY!

6

DON'T KNOW HOW LONG HE'S BEEN THERE,
BUT I HAVE TO BELIEVE,
SINCE HE SEEMS VERY COMFORTABLE,
HE'LL LIKELY NEVER LEAVE.

I WARNED MY LETTER CARRIER
TO PLACE MY MAIL WITH CARE,
BECAUSE I HAVE A TENANT
WHO CHOSE TO RESIDE THERE.

UNITED STATES
POSTAL SERVICE

I THINK I'LL NAME HIM NORBERT,
UNLESS I CALL HIM JAKE,
AND HOPE HE WON'T GET BOTHERED
BY MY GARDEN'S GARTER SNAKE.

12

HE'S REALLY VERY HANDSOME -
BRIGHT GREEN WITH HAZEL EYES,
AND, FRANKLY, I AM THANKFUL
THAT MY MAIL'S DEVOID OF FLIES!

IF NORBERT GETS MUCH BIGGER,
I'LL ADD A SECOND FLOOR.
A LETTERBOX WITH BALCONY,
AND MAYBE A FRENCH DOOR.

PERHAPS HE'LL HAVE A FAMILY.
THEY'LL NEED A BUS FOR SCHOOL.

18

SCHOOL BUS
Reptile Preparatory

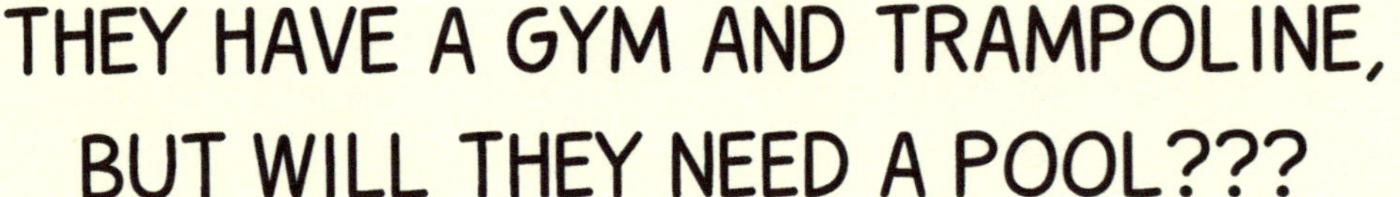

THEY HAVE A GYM AND TRAMPOLINE,
BUT WILL THEY NEED A POOL???

WHO KNEW I'D BE A LANDLORD?
SO MANY THINGS TO PLAN!
CAN LIZARDS SIGN A ONE-YEAR LEASE?
WILL THEY NEED A DOORMAN??

22

LEASE
The tenants known as NORBERT LIZARD hereby agrees to rent the premises located at 123 GECKO LANE for the rental fee of $0 for the month for the term of 1 year
LESSEE
LESSOR
Master

RESPONSIBILITIES ABOUND!
DO I NEED TO ADD A LOCK?
DO THEY NEED SECURITY, A LAWN AND A SIDEWALK?

Master

I'M OFF TO SPEAK WITH NORBERT
SO THERE CAN BE NO DOUBT
THAT HE'S A HAPPY RENTER.
NO NEED; NORBERT'S MOVED OUT!

THE END

It´s time to color

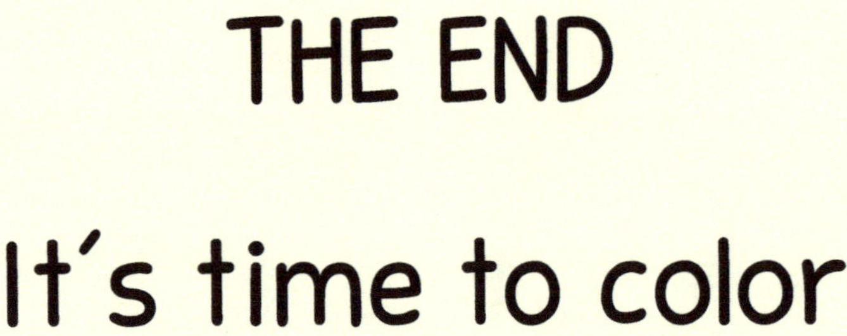

United States
Postal Service

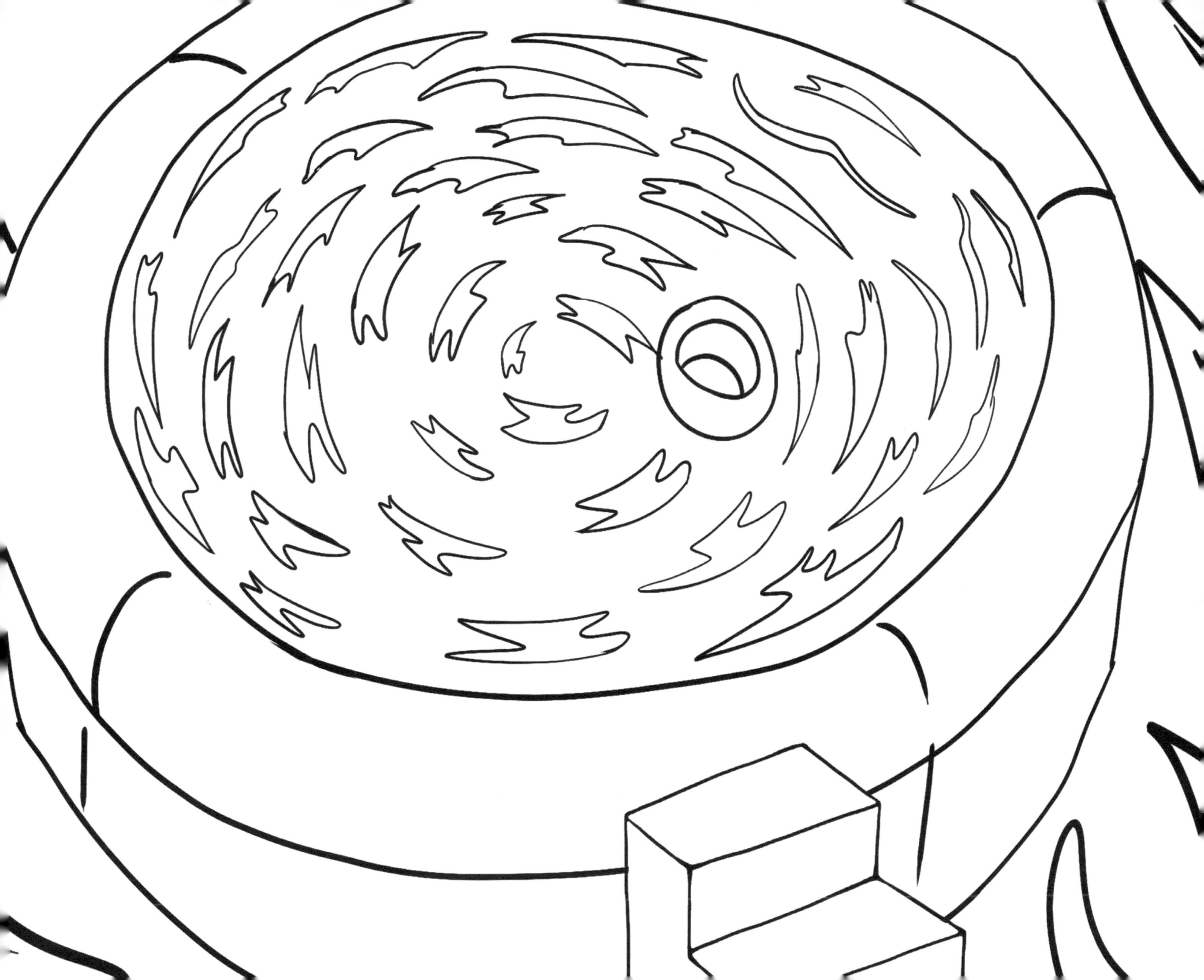

LETTER

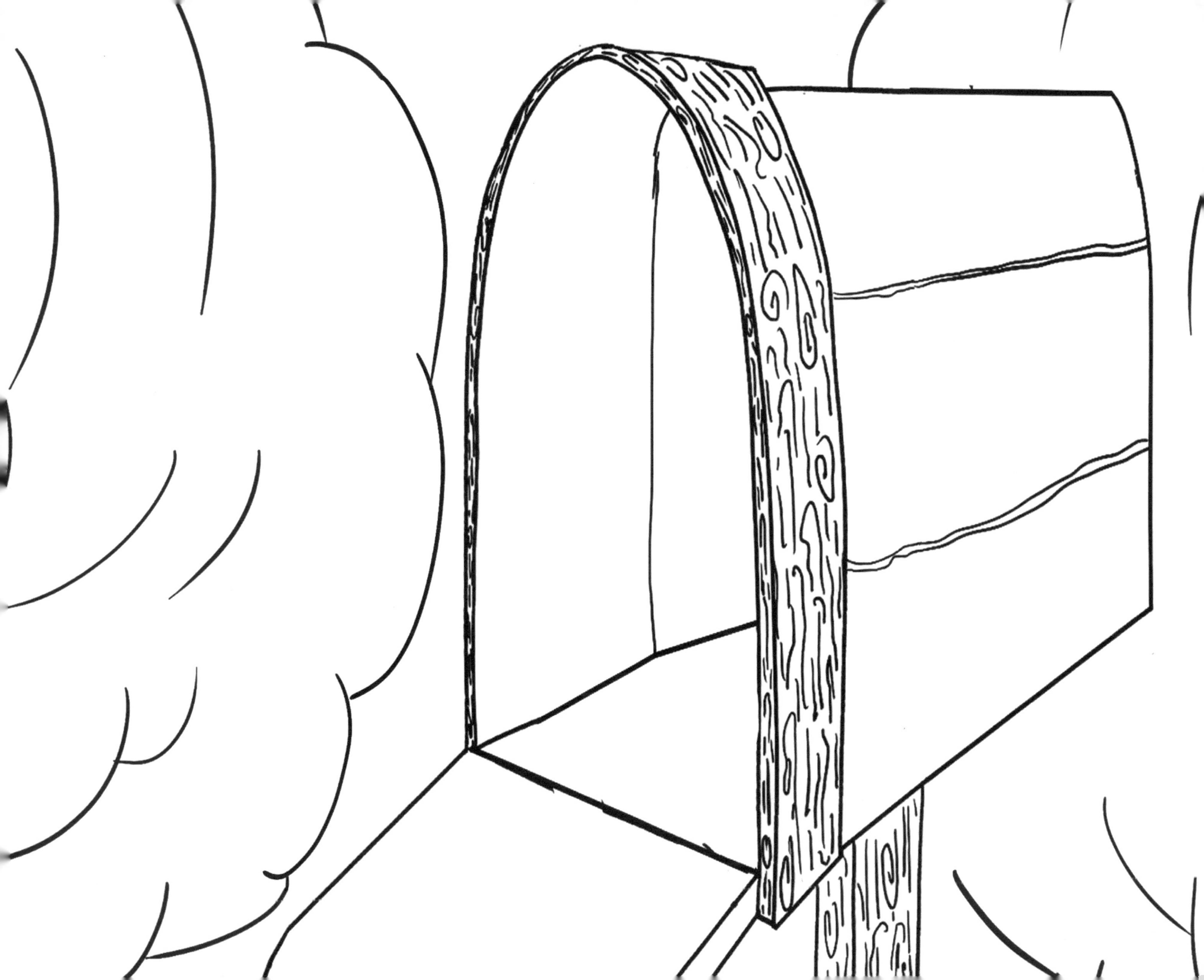